Wash Me On Home, Mama

Wash Me On Home, Mama

Pete Najarian

REGENT PRESS
Berkeley, California

Copyright © 1978, 2018 by Pete Najarian

Paperback
ISBN 13: 978-1-58790-457-8
ISBN 10: 1-58790-457-8

E-Book
ISBN 13: 978-1-58790-458-5
ISBN 10:1-58790-458-6

Library of Congress Catalog Number: 9781587904585

Originally published by Berkeley Poets Workshop and Press
ISBN 0-9-17658-10-8
Cover design by the author.

This printing of this book was originally funded bv a Grant
from the National Endowments of the Arts

Manufactured in the U.S.A.
Regent Press
Berkeley, California
www.regentpress.net

"Wash me on home, mama"
— Song of the Kelp.

Earth! Those beings living on your surface
none of them disappearing, will all be transformed.

— FROM *Myths and Texts* by Gary Snyder

You are so young, so before all beginning, and I want to beg you,
as much as I can, dear sir, to be patient toward all that is unsolved
in your heart and to try to love the *questions themselves* like
locked rooms and like books that are written in a very foreign
tongue. Do not now seek the answers, which cannot be given
you because you would not be able to live them. And the point
is, to live everything. *Live* the questions now. Perhaps you will
then gradually, without noticing it, live along some distant day
into the answer.

— FROM *Letters To A Young Poet* by Rilke

I am not a home. I am these rooms of my longing like the waiting rooms of a ferry station way out in the boondocks where no one rides the ferry anymore, that round chubby boat bobbing over the waves to the rhythm of a tuba, the patient tuba who always sat in back of the orchestra until one day someone wrote a song especially for his solitude, The Song of Tuba The Ferryboat, *pumping across the water beyond the Golden Gate where the soft coastal hills roll into the white and emerald sea... I am not happy. I am a man struggling, always fighting. I am a woman who reaches out and yearns for the opening of her dark walls that the birds of her heart may fly into the outside. I am a man driven by his own eyes. I am a wounded woman without a child. A man who can never say yes. A woman wandering to find a secret. A man who hates women. A woman behind locked doors. Unhappy men and women rebuilding engines, sewing zafus, trying to be great and simple with college degrees and job recommendations blowing in the wind as we run a few scams and hustle to Montana and New Mexico. 0 my people, in the middle of life we make ripples in the spawn and none of them remain. Where is the ferry, the fat red and blue boat that is a baby's washtub sailing on the waves of happiness? Does it appear on the horizon? Call to it and signal that we may hear again the joyful song of Tuba, the awakened one.*

But no, before I can sing I must cry. And tell again another story while we wait to leave for the other shore.

Here then are the people inside me as they were years ago when I lived in Berkeley, California. As I begin to look at them they become like the lemons and the pineapple on the counter by the sink, different patterns, things, future Buddhas, and yet all one, all together in their separate rooms.

First comes Dominic, my bald dreamer, who grew a beard in his mountain retreat and did not shave it when he came back to the commune in the flatlands. Now among the others he tries once more to join hands and break bread at the long table in the giant kitchen. After lunch he cleans up neatly (for he is one of the neat ones) and then drives the truck to the dump. The truck is loaded with the rubble of plaster from the wall e demolished yesterday. He knocked the wall down to open the space upstairs in this big old house that was once three separate apartments.

DOMINIC

We inherit space and fill it with our lives and our furniture, a long printer's table scavenged from a bankruptcy, a bumpy sofa leftover from a grandma, flea-market lamps, garage-sale refrigerator, and scrapwood benches worn smooth and polished by everyone's sweaty buttocks-things that will inherit everyone's death. A cock roach crawls along the sink, ventures across the faucet, finds a precipice and retreats. How has this place come to be here, this labyrinth of pipes and wires, water and gas in and out from stone and macadam, telephone and electricity stretching from where, arteries and veins of what wanderers-? Follow the line all the way back and find the point, aperture of the primal cause.

By the road to the dump low-tide, semi-circle of a tire and the willets picking in the mud, coots and gulls in the inlet, and the tall solitary egret delicately white amid debris. And then more gulls, gulls, an apocalypse of cawing gulls as Dominic stopped at the booth and paid the little round man of faded flannel and a baseball cap, and then entered the hills of garbage covered with new grass. In fifty years five hundred acres of land, land from the refuse of our lives buried beneath what would become another city extending into the bay, every day more and more, the giant wheels of a dinosaur tractor crushing our history into water, the plaster of walls and broken concrete adding to mountains of tons of knick knacks, baby carriages, chairs, pencils ... take an inventory: how many millennia did it take to shape metal and glass, conjure plastic and print words we now flip into the bay as easy as a booger of snot while the gulls screech over another desolation? And who will live on top of all our mistakes? Shove them all down into the pit under the crying frenzy of gulls and then bury them, bury them all like the flaming sunset, bury them and start all over again saving the screws, nails, hinges to build all over again believing another life will be better. And so Dominic dreamed of a small comer of the universe where he could start. He wandered to the side and with a scar between his eyes examined bits and pieces of metal and wood that might be useful. Waste nothing. Work hard, struggle and fight. Like a beaver, his life of work and more work. Post-scarcity gatherer who would build a future with leftovers, a vision of not anywhere he knew but had to believe in, Carbuncle, he would call his new home Carbuncle, in memory of Marx's boils, pus and rage against the beast he had grown to hate as he hated his past and all the shitheads wallowing in money. Like a beaver he never stopped moving, munching twigs and bark and building dams as if he could hold back just for a moment the flow of pain. All the fights, all the marches, all the cheap wine and coffee and cigarettes and nights after nights of endless strategy, and still it was not enough. But it was done, and now he would be quiet and work in silence, step by step like Lenin retreating to a library to figure things out. His library would be a little garrison in the middle of the city. A fort. One fort leading to another until thousands of forts lay across the wilderness. Soon there would be a bee-hive, a printing press, a kiln, a studio, crocks of beer, tools, wood, clothes, furniture, food, food for everyone, always. In mounds of wattle where the nibbling beavers would settle cozily into each other and get drunk by a warm hearth. And all the bits and pieces of our lives would fill a city of man like a vast alchemy of dream-stuff and play.

But Naomi has another passion. Each of my people has a different passion. She met Dominic in People's Park when the park first began and they dug and planted, she for the plants and he for the park. That seemed like a long time ago. Their romance. And when they first moved in here they shared the same room. But she sleeps alone now. 'She's been sleeping alone since he returned from the mountains. But then again she's slept alone most of her life. And in the morning she hurries to the garden. She's in the garden most of the time.

NAOMI

She tilted her head back and let the sunshine bathe her like a woman of the jungle. Oh to let it feed her flesh as it would seep into the garden in which she stands like a child with a mother, the afternoon full of her freckles and red hair, red as the color of chestnut, pomegranate, and manzanita, and as warm as wine. She wanted it, the warmth of the color of her hair which never spread over the pale complexion of her skin. She wiggled her fingers into the soil. Call it soil, dirt, or recycled shit, but the black under her fingernails was not unclean, and the odor of ammonia was better than deodorant. She wanted health, to feel her body shine again like those farm summers of her childhood. She wanted chickenshit on the porch and the odor of hay. She wanted it not as a vacation but every day, dirt, sloppiness, shloshiness, a mush of life churning, seething, and forever red. To be clean, a body rid of all test tube profits, clean of what was not even worthy to be called shit or piss but was a cancer spoon-fed into her blood in the blasphemy of nutriment. She would fight the poison with tomatoes and eggs, splatter the face of chemicals with seeds and yolk, protoplasm against death. With her sweaty hairy friends she'd bring the farm back, a food conspiracy to bring dirt into the town. She went forth to battle the rats that were invading the compost. She had built a new box in the corner of the garden . Now she had to line it with tin so the rats couldn't eat through the wood. And then move all the compost from the old box which was too close to the house . She spread t corrugated sheets of tin in the driveway and cut them with the big sheers. Then she fitted the pieces along the sides of the box, inserting them at least two feet below the level of the ground or the rats would dig and come up from underneath. She nailed the tin tight with roofing nails. And now she shoveled the compost from the old box and dumped it into the new one. Into the wheelbarrow went the history of meals. Shovel by shovel she lifted and dumped all campaigns, small planet recipes, the meat-guilt of vegetarian penance, rebellious pork-chop bones, defeated corners of the refrigerator, ignored leftovers, ambitious dinners that burned or exploded, rice, egg shells, spoiled raw vegetables, cooked vegetables, moldy bread, moldy cheese, moldy jam, green disgusting moldy fruit, corn cobs, melon rinds, tea leaves, worms, sawdust, dirt, the asparagus-piss and rotten-egg stench of decay, a mesmerizing pile of weird colors, reptile green, death white, sensual black, clotted red, food for food.

In the evening under the quilt, with the dog curled asleep and snoring at the foot of her bed, she cuddled into the warmth of a big fat simple novel, a bunch of people and history, a plot of life she entered like a child into the folds of time, war and peace. The Modern Library Giant filled her little hands as she lapped the sentences phrase by phrase feeding her imagination by the low light of the lamp over her shoulder, her loneliness in abeyance. She paused, her eyes suddenly out of focus, seeing double as she remembered her childhood curled on the rug, her ear to the console radio listening to the *Life of Riley.* How wonderful people were, families of people. There would be a large bucolic space, warm golden shafts of light through high shade trees, and all the people she had ever loved would be there and she would slip into them and swim between their bodies. Natasha would eventually be with Pierre. She knew that. After a thousand pages and twenty years Natasha would be with Pierre. It would all work out. But Sonya, poor Sonya, was there no one for Sonya? When the dog wants love he wags his tail and someone pets him. It was as simple as that. To learn how to wag her tail. And he would come. Come, oh my Dominic, come lie with me and by my love. With a child and all of us here.

— A baby, I want a baby.

She shut the light and shut her eyes and fell asleep hugging herself for protection against the night.

And Marian? When Naomi suggested to her that they all live together she said, "Yes, we must try." And so began the many meetings about money and who had a rich aunt to borrow from, an inheritance to tap, a car to sell, or savings to gamble on the wild chance that it would be possible for all of them to live together under the same roof. And so the strange words, escrow and mortgage. And so this enormous old house on the corner with a row of garages and a giant garden, a chicken coop and a duck yard and a rabbit pen. And a woodpile piling higher and higher, and an ecology shed overflowing with bottles and cans. And clogged toilet bowls and broken pipes. And three dogs and two cats and four cars two of which never run and three garbage cans three of which are always full. And a communal living room that was once a barber shop and now looks like a barber shop with everything gone except a few chairs and an old calendar. And so Marian comes down the kitchen in the morning and then goes over to one of the garages which she converted into a studio for her loom.

MARIAN

Everyone has a rhythm and the need of finding it, so that all together we may improvise with the great dance of the universe, music instead of noise. The morning begins with the rooster, rattle of bamboo in the breeze, someone's step-step off to work down the dark stairs, coughs and groans, and a child yelling. In the bathroom a powerful shit mixes with the sweet mint of toothpaste. The air is filled with the aftermath of dreams, cold draughts from the world of night. The long corridor and the stairs down to the kitchen become a tunnel to the day. The same kitchen as last night's dinner but now a different light streams across the table. She would sit down and eat but for the cigarette butts, banana peel, half-eaten food, spilled milk, and the noise growing louder and louder inside her head. She balanced herself carefully so that the thin pin inside her head•that held everything together would not slip out and make her fly wildly around the room like a panicked bird. She walked across the dew-wet quiet of the garden and over to her garage where she could be alone. Albinoni on the stereo and she went about watering her plants, her long purple and violet caftan in a slow dance from maidenhair to asparagus ferns to simple wandering Jew, all her melancholy irrelevant to the green silence of their peace, oblivious to everything but the mystery of new leaves. She smiled from deep inside the convent of her dreams. Her life: for ever longing. Like the deer, symbol of longevity, long-lasting and yet never filled, always moving, looking for home. She heard her self in music, the deep reed and light step of strings, seeking to fill the space beyond like undulating curls of incense in the home coming light through the woven curtain. Music, or painting and the time inside a canvas, forever pulsing, lambent upon the areas of darkness, time as seen by light or was it light itself that mysteriously moved in measure, was time light and light time in the faces and landscapes of her private museum? Play its theme upon the loom and do not think, but shuttle and pedal as if playing keys, fingering the bright wool in counterpoint to breath and memory. There are no answers, only needs: to be, to fill, make hole, consummate. But not to talk about, her own private wilderness, entering it like Sacajawea leading two men up river, father and brother into the green mystery of her secret treasures, the deep seclusion of fern and moss, soft rain from the compassionate sky, earth fed by paternal clouds, grey to form green, father on top of mother, fecund love. From inside the window she watched the light through the avocado tree accompanied by the forest lullaby of far eastern music, the morning of the world. Oh her world is rich here inside her womb, her loom room overflowing with colors like stained glass. Come and see, come play with her and and she may open if you are gentle the door to her ... home, what happened to it? Is it this now, with delicate china and cockroaches and a courtyard of marigolds and garbage? How could she make it glimmer and reflect the dreams of her yearning? Home, yes, but oh could it not be more of a temple than a fort?

For Sam however, all that mattered was that his wife Marian love him. "Please love me," he wanted to say. Instead he said, "Okay, we'll move in and have separate rooms." It was either this or separate apartments. But after so many years he couldn't let go of her, nor could she tear herself away from him. It took several months before she finally moved into her own room.

MARIAN AND SAM

Rearranging her life, she put her bed in one corner, desk in the other, rocking chair by the desk, bureau by the bed, books next to the bureau, plants next to the books, Durer's Rabbit over the bed, and all the knick-knacks neatly in place, the fine oriental cloissone case of Zuni jewelry, the Dundee Marmalade jar of freeze-dried wildflowers, two tiny ivory elephants, a wicker box of sewing stuff, her special saw and hammer she did not want in the tool shed because it was always getting lost, her work-boots and sandals, dresses and overalls, all in proper order, all the elegant and precious, funky and second- hand talismans and mementos gathered and gleaned from friends, flea-markets, forests, and the sea, an agate here, a handblown vase there, an ancient tin Murad Cigarette box full of old postcards, a pewter cup of bleached bones from Baja, all the remnants of her history that each year she kept shed ding and growing, every scar and spoil, studied and adored with her own desperate yearning for something permanent and real, and then recycled by garage-sale and potlatch, her life as an antique shop, everything now dusted and straightened and fitted and smoothed and folded and tacked and readied in a new room, a new space. She hung the woven curtains, nailed the tapestry next to the window, lit a stick of frankincense, and stood in the doorway picking her nose: HER SPACE.

He would enter tip-toed. He would speak softly in this sanctuary of her tears and solitude. He would respect her pride and be gentle and considerate to her hatred and understand her anger and let her cut his balls off. Because he was afraid of that room. Because he liked it, he thought it was beautiful.

She came out of the shower naked, springing on her arches, with an imaginary string holding her head high and her back straight, her hair in a snood, droplets beading her body, beautiful body, lovely breasts, soft shiny hair on her cunt, Apollonian next to his kinkiness. He wanted to fuck her from behind as he studied her buttocks. He would ask her to crouch on her bed and let him hold her breasts and raise her cheeks to his cock and he would come up from underneath. Instead he said:

— Hey!
— What?
— Is there any hot water left?
— Sure, there's plenty.

Her soft purple and red panties dangle on the doorknob. He put his nose in the crotch of the smooth nylon. Ah, sex! He stepped into the shower with a hard-on, his golden key that would open the door to her paradise. She didn't want it anymore, and he watched it shrink back into all the rejections of his life. Water would soothe them away. He stared at all the different plastic bottles on the shelf of the communal bathroom. Herbal shampoo, Dr. Bonner's 100% natural cocoanut-olive-peppermint oils, Johnson's Baby Shampoo, Ivory Soap, glycerin soap, oatmeal soap, lavender, strawberry, and avocado to wash away all the shame of every time he knocked on a door to ask: Please let me fuck you. He lathered his balls, asshole, and armpits, and from deep in his longing for every woman he ever wanted to enter he yelled *Che ha detto ii Medico* from *LA Boheme:*
Mimi! Oh, Mimi!

Meanwhile Buster. Buster always meanwhile, the in-between friend who hides behind the wrinkles of his phony smile. He moved in too because why not? The rent is cheap, and in one of the garages he can build a workspace and make believe he's an artist. Here with the others he won't have to be alone anymore. And yet he's always alone, trying to hide from the angel of death on his shoulder.

BUSTER

Three duck eggs scrambled gently with a little dill, a baguette of sour dough and a heavy cup of strong French Roast as he looked over the garden and enjoyed himself. Indian summer a dominion of weeds, the tall broccoli sprouting yellow flowers. The first cigarette of the day rumbled his belly toward the pleasure of the john. He shat a big rich brown heap of yesterday's life, yawned a great bone-cracking cosmic sigh, and stared in the luminous mirror:

— Hello, Meatball!

Flesh the Great Beatie would one day roll into a ball of dung. And now what should he do with his life? Be could enjoy himself, or he could get a job. The Venerable Bum, a big mound of hair on top of bulk. You want to hug him as if he were a friendly bear, gentle strength swaying softly barefoot across the garden to his garage next to the duck yard and the chicken house. He poured himself a second cup of coffee from the old gray porcelain percolator on the pot-belly stove and then settled into the raw clean-smelling ply wood desk and the pleasure of freshly sharpened pencils. And once again mesmeric doodles flowed from his nimble fingers, the enormous talent and prodigious indolence like twenty pounds of dictionary flowing patiently with the soft refrain: *it will all work out, it will all work out, it will all work out.* And all the tears behind the twinkling eyes were held inside by little pleasures that locked his heart.

Later on he decided to do a little work. Tacked to the old gray wood of the tool shed smiled a print of a Chinese scroll, two Sung monkeys playing in the branches of a juniper tree. Buster grabbed the shovel, the pick, and the machete, and went to the duck yard. Clearing the blackberry bush for the ducks he loved he thought of settlers in wildnerness. With his arms bleeding in

the sun he thought of Berkeley as a wilderness, the heart of the
Beast. And thinking of Guevara he transformed his work into
an adventure . Sucking delicious blood and sweat from where
the thorns had cut his arms, he whacked at the bramble and with
each whack of the machete he imagined a jungle: whack for
Guevara, whack for satchidananda, whack for everybody,
and whack for the ducks.

Enough bush in the back for plenty of berries, and clearing
this one in the center would leave space for a pond, the big
pool of duck happiness. But the bramble was tight, woven with
generations, and no end or beginning to untie the knot, no way
to clear it except by slicing, slicing vine by vine like a pioneer
in a forest. The butter flies applauded with a ballet over the
fence. Finally he had it all down and rolled it tumble by tumble
to the truck. Now with the pick he ripped into the white pulpy
roots that gripped tight to the soil, generations fat from their
undisturbed sucking. He smashed and killed them, his hands
burning, biceps swelling. He sighed:

— Ah, it feels good.

The two mallards, the muscovy, and the six white Pekings
stared at him not with curiosity but fear, their steady
unblinking eyes wide like lunatics tortured with paranoia.

—It's for you guys, you quack-quacks. A big pool. Cool
water. Happiness.

They kept staring at him standing there with the pick in his
hand, all their wings clipped, each one held captive in his
prison.

And now to complete my gestalt is Daphne, the youngest member and the only one who works "out there," commuting between here and the world outside the driftwood fences of the garden. She moved in after telling her old boyfriend to go fuck himself, and then she got the job at the Post Office she'd been waiting for. She'll be here for a while, but not for long.

DAPHNE

In autumn the scoters and coots are joined by canvasback, golden eye, bufflehead, merganser, and pintail. Day by day the sun sets further and further south and sinks behind the Golden Gate. And on one late afternoon when the heavy clouds were drifting away, Daphne could see it floating between the pylons of the bridge, a red balloon dropping in a cradle. During the rain that day she ate her lunch in a relay box, stuffing peanut butter and jam in her cheeks like a child in fruit-crate. But at the end of her route the rain had stopped and she studied the sky and its shifting light, gray, then gold as scud clouds gibed with the sun. Wet wine-red leaves of the plum trees and leaves of the liquid amber, cerise and yellow, decorated the sidewalks like mosaic. So many trees, elm, Chinese Elm, buckeye, cedar, incense cedar, redwood, camphor, ginkgo, bay, banya-banya, juniper, palm ... there were more different trees in Berkeley than there were people. Often she couldn't see the difference between freak, straight, poor and not so poor black, who were always changing as the city itself changed from the Free Speech Movement to communes to ashrams to people living alone again as they did before the war. She had come here a girl eager for college and found herself six years later eating peanut-butter and jam in a mail-box. She was tired, her bag full of letters marked NO LONG ER AT THIS ADDRESS. Berkeley had become a flyway to her migratory generation. She hopped in her little three-wheel scooter and zipped down the hill to Telegraph Avenue. At twenty-four, in gray sweater and skirt, she felt old and wise, and for old time's sake stopped in the Mediterranean Cafe to sit by the window and watch the people go by. "Tell me about **FSM,**" a friend once asked her. **"FSM** was I was a virgin and we stayed up all night and I met my first lover." And in the Mediterranean dirty raincoats and leotards talked of *The Myth of Sisyphys* and *Jules and Jim*. And everyone had come back from the South, but no one was allowed to talk under the sycamores in Sproul Plaza. She never did get a degree. Instead lots of leaflets, acid, tripping and canvassing, marching among burning draft cards and jungle music in streets of flowers, of pellets, of incense and broken bottles ... until someone turned her on to yoga through whom she met someone who took her to her first encounter group through whom she met someone who led her to someone who one and on into the labyrinth ... until People's Park became the last stop and all the pieces of people settled into the great calabash, pot-pouri of Gurdjieff, Guevara, Shambala, scientology, electoral politics, liberals with long hair, radicals with short hair, food stamps, falaffel, bioenergetics, motorcycles ... sucking her into a cornucopia of bummer and illumination ... and now what was there to do, where was there to go? A young black man sat at her table and she looked away, angry at him, expecting him to come on to her. But he didn't, and looking back into the cafe she saw that all the other tables were filled and he had nowhere else to sit. How do the seeds find their places? From the wind and the wandering of animals, and somewhere is home but staying is nowhere.

Before going to bed she wrote her desires on the shopping list taped to the refrigerator door. Under *toilet paper, orange juice,* and *dog-food* she printed in thick yellow crayon:

    FROG **HEAVEN**

    BEAR WALLOW

    AND FIVE ACRES

    OF QUIVERING ASPEN

And that night while she lay in bed she heard that strange sound from where she couldn't figure out until yes, yes, it was the geese from Canada, flying over her bedroom on their way south, the great V honking especially for her, blowing like a hundred little tubas pumping across the sky, breathing in and out the song of their journey, the name of their essence, *hamsa,* the symbol of Brahma, the god of creation, *hamsa-saham, this am I-I am this, this am I-I am this.* And when in her pajamas she rushed outside to see them they had passed and the scattered wisps of night cloud were like their echoes.

Dominic also has a garage along with Marian and Buster. He converted his into a little shop for his woodwork. He's been staying in it a lot these days, regressing to his old habit of being alone like an old shoemaker all day by himself with a scratchy little radio and the strong smell of glue. Naomi told him she might be pregnant. That's all he needed to hear. After dinner every night he goes to his garage, turns on the little radio, surrounds himself with wood, and gets drunk.

DOMINIC

He sat in drifts of sawdust and curly shavings and sipped his whiskey and withdrew into the little holes and pegs of his Morris chair, the night sky chanting flamenco with the illuminated clouds of a Spanish turbulence rising over the hills. He sanded his chair and drank to the bones of a revolution. The night drew colder and he fed his little stove with scraps of old lathing and studs. The thought of broken walls led to broken pipes leading to bills which led to babies. He poured another glass and inserted a peg in its hole. Naomi wanted a baby.

— I want one, she said.
— And what about our life? he said.
— What about our life? she said. What do you think our life is about?

Do you know what it feels like, he asked the whiskey, what is feels like to make a chair? The reason I'm such a good person, he said to the red glow in the stove, why I'm so wonderful is because I love wood. I mean, he said to the apricot tree black against the night blue sky, do you know what it feels like to find old wood and peg it back together to make a chair? To take old life, he said to her orange window, to take old life and make it new? To take this life, he said to the crucifix of the telephone pole in the street, this life that has fallen apart and build it back together again? But, he said looking nowhere into the darkness of the garden, I don't want no fucking baby, I don't want no instant meaningfulness, no. Drunk, he plunged into his dreams. With all the sentiment of Dewar's White Label he watched the movie in his mind, roofs opening with skylights, streets flowering into playgrounds, bicycles on every comer, all chimney pots painted bright colors, sidewalks shining with mosaic, utopia, like a child building a fort out of fruit-crates and old linoleum, our home in the comer of the universe ... I want to build, you go make your own baby, go add another to all the swollen bellies sucking dry and withered tits, whose eyes burn my eyes with their hunger. I am my own baby, my own starving. I was my mother's baby and look what happened. You were your mother's baby and look what happened. And you went to make another one of this bullshit? I know what you want. You want that stupid contented smile of a pregnant woman who pisses a hundred times a day and carries her belly like it was her masterpiece. One more masterpiece to four billion masterpieces. Oh but your's will be different. Your little angel will be another Buddha sucking his thumb under the Bo tree.

He went into the house and sank into the sofa in the eerie demonic red and green glow of the fish-tank that was like an empty three a.m. saloon on the waterfront. And he gazed at the fish, rainbow, angel, gourami, and Chinese Algae flowing back and forth, bumping into the glass like the phantoms in his skull, the Big Oscar blowing bubbles in the corner. And he fell asleep, and he dreamed of a demon sneaking up through the basement. And upstairs Naomi was dreaming and the others were dreaming and the dogs and the cats were dreaming and outside the rabbits and the chickens and the ducks were dreaming and all the dreams floated into the hundred thousand other dreams of the city, into a cloud purling into all the other clouds of all the other cities, a milky ocean of fears and fulfillment. And only the fish were not dreaming as they swam back and forth bumping into the glass like a little fetus in a belly.

Marian and Sam have a six year old boy , Theo, who's in school now. He is not in my story yet. He is the child who is father to our future. He runs in and out with his friends on the block and so far still has one foot in paradise, or maybe it's just a toe. Marian clings to him and Sam tries to hide from him lest he see his father's pain . Without him Marian is not Marian, and with him she is more mother than Marian. And even before him when she was little Marian she was not just Marian but Marian the daughter, the granddaughter, the niece, cousin, and sister. She was never Marian without a family and yet she was never Marian with one.

MARIAN

Rain! And the dry hills will turn green. The first rains of autumn clear grime from the glass, shine the streets, make mud in the garden. Rain to the music of Mozart, dripping notes from the sky, gathering everyone indoors. When it rained when we were small we got half day from school. We would come home to cookies and milk and be inside and sit by the window and watch the rain blur and mystify the things outside. Now, here in the kitchen, Naomi at the stove in overalls and pigtails like a modern pioneer is brilliant under the electric light in the dark grey morning. Catch the moment like a dry brush, Daphne on her day off flipping pancakes dehanchment to the mixing bowl, Buster and Sam sitting at the table like card players, Dominic at the window looking up at the thunder. Now overlay the present with an old brown photograph from an immigrant ghetto, family and family stuffed into railroad rooms, congregating in loud kitchens of gossip and complaints. Now cut to the silence of an old woman asleep in front of her television, her sons and daughters scattered across the country in pastel houses surrounded by empty lawns. But return to the moment, grandchildren returning to poverty and congestion in the fever of nostalgia. Marian, her hair tied in a red kerchief like a peasant, sang an old folksong from her father's childhood:

> *nuss i denn muss i denn muss i denn*
> *zum stadtele hinaus*
> *und du mein schatz bleibst hier*

When it rains we stay inside and make ourselves cozy, bullshitting and hanging out. Rain is the weather for daytime fucking, for lying in bed and telling stories. But she wanted to be alone. With the rain bringing memories. In her room she embroidered patches on her pants, the same stitch she had been using how many years now, as if she were sewing her own mummy cloth. The rain did not stop, crackling and dripping all morning and noon against the window pane. Her son in school and all the chores done, she closed her door and continued her feather stitch, repeating it as if it were a string of prayer beads. How many years now since she was free, or was she ever? What was wrong with her, why was she never satisfied, what did she really want? The thought of her son pulled at her shirt.

That year in Europe when he stayed with his father in London and she hitch-hiked through Germany to visit her grandmother she could have kept going, she could have never come back, her baby calling her back as she went further and further into the Schwarzwald, the old truck-driver so pleased with her fluency he treated her to that delicious *schinkenbroat* in the *warmgasthaus,* and she was not afraid ... yes she wanted a child and yes she was too young to have a child ... for was she not happy alone in her grandmother's house full of old apples and could she not have gone further into and through the Black Forest ... she had never been to Austria and she had never been to Persia and no she had never been to India ... and when was she ever truly alone and free, her baby calling her back : Mommy! Mommy ! ... what she loved most in the world holding her down ... *Space, Space, Space* kept ticking against the glass of her closed room ... Craving, The Seamstress, winding a tight and deadly coccoon around her wings.

Sam on the other hand is always Sam, with son, without son, with wife, without wife, family or no family, he is always poor little Sammy. With a worthless M.A. in one pocket and food stamps in the other. Maybe his mother was to blame. Or his father. Why he was such a jerk-off. Or maybe it was money. Or capitalism. Or genes. The world in which he always failed.

SAM

Cold sunsets called the coming of winter like a moaning koto. Behind the Gate grey horizons brought gloomy days of sore throat and headache, and the leafless plum trees became old threadbare and crooked hermits. Cold grisly rain sharpened the rheumy claws of flu and stiffness, rain and more rain. He didn't see the sun for days and bumped into everyone, snapping and fighting as if he were in a cage. Maybe money was the answer, why he was so worthless. Maybe he could get help from a foundation, a grant, an endowment for what he could call the failure of his life, a sociological study, an economic program, an anthropological expedition. Money would save him and bring her back to him. Fuck money and all those who have it. Only the big muscle in his belly from his stomach to his balls could ease his rigid pelvis and make for *wu-wei* and *sich Lassen.* But he did not let go, he tightened his ass and locked his knees and hated his life and his wife with every knot in his neck. And all the memories of love, all the pictures from the family album of happiness, mother, father, and child, filled his heart with suffering. The thought of her cunt filled him with rage punching a hole in the wall, breaking her face into blood and teeth. Better when she broke a chair over his back, hit him in the head with her wooden shoe, let her tear him apart and it would be better than the knife of her shrivelled indifferent face that stabbed his eyes with all her stinginess and frigidity. Could this ugly douchbag be the same woman who once kissed him in the darkness, his wet satisfied prick snug in her ass, his arm around her holding her lovely tit in his hand like a bird, his chest warm and tight to her back, their flesh fitting into each other glued and moist? Oh her smell, her special smell, his darling wife, her eyes so sincere, whispering to him with Vivaldi and Joan Baez: I love you, dear heart, my darling Sam, I love you. My darling douchbag. Her cunt, that once loomed in his life like a religious vision, now became his death, filling him with memories of all the women he ever hated, all the cheerleaders and majorettes twirling their batons and pumping their fists yelling: fuck me! fuck me! and the fucking bimbo he shaved his face bloody for and she says with that shit-eating smile: I want to be your *friend,* Sam, can't we just be *friends?* all the women with the face that launched a thousand ships whom he could never fuck because he was desperate, the woman-sickness that consumed his life, the female of the species carrying her ass like a mandrill looking over her shoulder and laughing : Sammy, Sammy the limp noodle. He lay crippled and defeated, his legs like polio, his neck like arthritis, his lungs like cancer, his face like palsy, his little prick like a blood clot in the brain. He wanted to die. Unable to breathe, racked by the chains of hatred and memory, he prayed for a thunderbolt to stab his lungs, slice him open from neck to groin, electrocute his eyes, and explode his brain into the wind. To die. To tear his life asunder. He became obsessed with the bridge, the best way to die. The beautiful flight. The Golden Gate that would become the last exit of his journey. Every day it waited on the horizon: a small paragraph in the Chronicle: an unidentified man, of no use to the world or his wife, became the 424th suicide of the Golden Gate Bridge yesterday morning. His disgusting body was found washed upon the beach with old bloody Kotex and stinky diaphragms. But one witness reported that the moment of his death justified all his suffering. He had parked his car on the green of the Presidio, ran with tremendous energy and passion through the cold and windy morning, reached the middle of the bridge, and without hesitation flung his arms open and leaped over the railing and cracked his life into a million stars.

Meanwhile Buster, though he's aware of the trouble between Marian and Sam and Dominic and Naomi, stays out of it. There are supposed to be group therapy sessions when everyone sits down together and talks it out. But they never work and he always wants to leave and take the dogs for a walk. Secretly he envied them their problems. He'd rather have a problem with a woman than no problem with no woman. But then, he was too lazy and tired and the dogs were always easier.

BUSTER

He took the dogs for a walk and they raced into the wonderful world of new piss and shit. He walked behind them, a backward guide to their unbounded joy. They went across the football field of the high-school and up Durant Street past all the churches and over to the University, the streets and trees wet and shiny in the aftermath of rain, the air clean and cold. And the dogs opened his head and straightened his back and he followed them. He found a spot by Sather Gate while they fucked around by the fountain, and he sat leaning against the stone balustrade and watched the women go by, sniffing with his eyes the legs, buttocks, and imagined vaginas in parade under the falling brown and yellow leaves of the sycamores: women, women everywhere. In half an hour he counted twenty-eight beautiful women pass through the gate. *Pig!* the spirit of the woman's movement whispered into his private beauty contest. He whispered back:

— I'm not a pig.

Surely woman is the pig, the fruitful and receptive womb. And how ugly they were when they were not beautiful. What could be more ugly than an ugly woman, old with long tits, bulging eyes, twisted fangs and a red flame-tipped tongue? And yet, he remembered, there was once an old fat wrinkled black woman in Harlem, chewing tobacco and spitting in a coffee can, with skin like an elephant's and as soft as a daffodil, and how much he loved her.

— I love women, I've always loved women.

He sat by the gate and yearned to kiss their lips and fuck them. But the Hare Krishna people? He watched them jingle and moan with their vapid eyes and pasty flesh . Nor were the street-people beautiful, deposited on the steps of the Student Union, Telegraph Avenue feeding into Sproul Plaza like hunger into a garbage can. Nor was the University beautiful, the dregs of progress, the card tables of various causes like beggars by a bank. The freckled gap-toothed preacher with his hair on fire and eyes burning like amphetamine, yelled to a crowd:

— Jesus Christ! Jesus Christ!

But the dogs carried on enjoying themselves sniffing assholes by the fountain.

They ran past, barking and nipping each other as he walked up Bancroft Way. They were so easy to please with odors everywhere. They passed the museum and he waved hello to Hans Hoffman and the Chinese landscapes and continued up and across Piedmont Avenue toward the School of the Blind, the ivy along the wall splashed bright red and green. The great pine tree on Derby Street swung out into the sky like an ideogram, a picture word of a strange language: dragon licks the sky in fellatio. The univere equals a giant fuck. Past the row of poplars and the old mossy fence, they entered the hills and he followed the dogs up the trail. The eucalyptus was pungent from the rain and the fresh mud and new stream of water curved into a hawk high across the canyon. And the ritual began again. Always with the light, long and almost palpable in the late afternoon, and trying to name *it,* to find the right word to hold *it* and fix *it* or at least describe *it* and how *it* charged every pebble, every twig, every wrinkle of mud with . . . what was *it,* what was the name of what he saw ... and finding no word, no way of connecting to what made the lupen and poppy so religiously purple and orange, he came to that place where . . . more than anything or anyone he loved his own eyes, and it was with his eyes that he tried to fuck the world, wanting to enter the call of birds and all the colors through the luxurious rays that speared

the hills just before sundown, wanting to cling to the pattern of
sage and yarrow, to embrace the secret of why the trees were
so beautiful and have it always and forever ... and yet, when
did he ever get near to even touching *it?* And then one day *it*
would be gone forever just as she whoever she was long before
he could remember went away and never returned, the power
that would plunge him into darkness, the light he spoke to as if
it could hear.

—— You won't let me touch you.

All I can do is look.
Fool said the sagebrush as he looked down below at the School of
the Blind, and all the blind children down there tapping the side
walk with their sticks, their eyes pinched black.

The dogs waited. The next hill was very steep and the ruddy
trail ascended into the vaulted dome of the sky. As he climbed
and panted, his breath opened his lungs and made way for the
surge of junk buried in his past, rising and filling his eyes with
pain as each step dug deeper into the bullshit of his life. At the
top his vision was blurred by all the crap in his skull and he
turned to stare at the huge grid of the city spread below the hills
like a target for a maniac bomber. Just as all colors become
an ugly grey when squished together, so too all those sounds
down there in the pan from Lake Merritt to Point Richmond,
from the campanile to the wharf, all the sounds of those million
people and their business and their struggles and their desires,
become an ugly moan in the grinding hum of the freeway like a
prayer wheel of misery. Polis. Necropolis. But here above it all
the hills were flaming in the sundown and a terrible calm hung
suspended in the breeze. And all the birds were singing, junco,
finch, towhee, and sparrow. And the kestrel hovered and cawed
in the canyon: killy, killy, killy. He entered the grove of the
cypress trees and the dogs followed him into what had become

his own private chapel. The gentle branches embroidered the light into a net of golden coins and icons, gold mingled with pips and needles, Coptic jewels and the world of green stars that were the moss. He sat in the cool cushion of loam and watched the dogs dig for the mole. The gossamer lace of cobwebs flung sparkles from the captured light and recalled all the chapels of his furious wandering, the peace offered to him by the angel of silence, that quiet garden in Florence, the stillness in Ravenna, the understanding Virgin that night at the Metropolitan, the cool somber glow that afternoon in Notre Dame, the Buddhist temple in the Fine Arts, the private mornings at the National Gallery, and all the sanctuaries to his fugitive pain. And as he cried he squeezed the tears, from deep in his darkness up into the treasure of his eyes, his eyes. What would the dogs do if they caught the poor soft mole with tiny feet and no eyes? Would they kill the little creature that gave them SQ_ much pleasure as they kept digging and stuffing their noses into the earth? The sun was dead. The light and the gold disappeared. The trees turned dark and cold. He could not defend himself. Now with his heart open from all the crying and his eyes washed clean and lucid, he once again felt the hand on his shoulder, the hand that always touched his left shoulder. And when he turned to look at the face of his death, it disappeared into the silence of the trees and the rocks.

The sky was now streaked cinnabar and purple, dragon's blood behind the Golden Gate. And the city below turned on its electric light and began to wave a veil of jewels like an undulating harem dance. Oh, to ease his head between her tits. And let her swallow his eyes once and for all, the knife of his eyes that see everything so clearly.

Daphne, however, is my hope. Daphne, my young Daphne, former cheer leader and fox, girlfriend and chick, who now punches her ann fuck-you and saves her money.

DAPHNE

She was curled half-asleep still in her work-clothes when the dinner-gong rang but no one was ever on time so why hurry? She pasted her eyes on the shreds of the ceiling and watched her body lie exhausted, her arms folded on her breasts like an angel, her innocent legs open across the bed. *I am sweet and delicate.* But her room was a garbage can of thirsty plants, staggering piles of paper backs, dirty clothes and dean clothes in scattered heaps like a free box, the half-finished curtain, the unplastered hole in the wall, the unfinished macramé, jewelry and the kitten all jumbled together like kindergarten. Why couldn't he get it together? Every week end she'd set her life straight and by Tuesday it was a mess, cigarette butts and ashes on the rug, a half-eaten apple in the plant box, cookie crumbles in the bed, the bed sheets only half on the mattress, and over it all the crooked frame of a print from the Cloisters, her beautiful unicorn. Delicate women in a clean studio weaving a neat and ordered world. How did delicacy develop? What law of survival formed frailty, small bones and timid muscles, centuries and centuries of breeding and cross-breeding for prettier and prettier and more delicate and more delicate possessions until all that was left seemed a flower to be admired and protected. Well fuck all that. Therefore she rolled her long princess hair into a bun, pulled on her boots, and clumped through the dark morning to stand among cigars and potbellies that bantered bad and boring jokes across the aisles. The chaste maiden amid G.I. Joe and Andy Capp. She liked it. And in those long hours shuffling and dealing letters into the little cubby-holes, her mind, once too big for her body, found rest in the routine of tying hundreds and hundreds of people together via the postal service. At ten o'clock she had her bundles tied and wheeled her bag into the streets, into the world waiting for letters . It needed her, her dirty hands, her aching back, her stinky socks. Here comes the Postlady! All the way from hopscotch and the small girl's corner of the schoolyard. Now into the world of coffee and doughnuts with *all* the husky boots and *Big Man* denim shirts, and a housewife waving from the window, and children staring at her as if she were somebody. She walked, she walked up and down the heavy streets as if she ere, yes, somebody, proving she didn't have to marry to be somebody, depend on Mr. Motor cycle and wash Captain Macho's underwear to be somebody. She came home tired. All of her hundred and ten pounds snuggled under the multicolored patch-quilt and she snored politely into the embroidered pillow like a child.

Naomi also likes to take the dogs for a walk and she usually goes down by the bay, parks by a jetty, and walks parallel to San Francisco and the Golden Gate Bridge and the coastal range across the horizon. The best time to go is at low tide at sundown after a clear day when the willets and the sandpipers pick shellfish along the, gleaming beach. Here she can be on the other side of the railroad tracks, on the other side of the freeway, at the edge of the tide that flows back to where the sun dies. Yes, she is pregnant and now she must decide whether or not to have an abortion.

NAOMI

A long tumble of rocks lined the beach along Frontage Road. She stood on one of them and spread-eagle she stretched her arms and hugged the water and the glorious horizon. And with one hand she touched the Bay Bridge and with the other touched Mt. Tamalpais way over there in Marin. Gracefully barefoot she tip-toed over the cool slimy stones that were buried in the sand in perfect pattern as if an old monk had spent his life arranging a path between rusty metal and driftwood and garbage. The dogs ran toward the willets, stopped short, circled, and rolled over crazy with space. Her beach, her beach despite the sign:

This is Private Property KEEP OFF
Berkeley PD. Ord.
2829-NS
The A.T . & S.F. Ry. Co.

She almost stepped on the head of a lamb or a donkey buried in the sand, its eye-sockets full of kelp . A few moons ago it was another kind of animal , and before that it was a seal. And with them the high tide delivered beer cans and plastic bags and deadly foam. The sea, our mother, vomiting death. On the other side of the Golden Gate it was clear and clean, but here in the bay it was an old fortune-teller spitting hair and bones. She didn't care anymore . However dirty, the waves would always yield treasure into the rocks, the rocks like old age, gold, purple, burnt sienna, umbra in the slant of sundown. As the dogs sniffed for rats she looked for pieces of wood and metal that could be woven into tapestry, beautiful chunks and scraps designed by worms and barnacles and the churning of the sea. She ignored the filth and stood upon a cluster of mussels and stared at the small waves rippling like long chords of music, the light glimmering across them like golden mail. An echo of foam bubbled pink across the sand. The stones darkened into

deeper and deeper green. And the shore became her magic
carpet, sailing into the easy blue of Venus and the moon . Then
suddenly a silhouette of dogs raced across the burnished copper
belly of the tide and a flock of gulls burst like firework in the
twilight . Here is our home where if we could harness ourselves
to the wings of our longing so too could we fly beyond the Gate
to where the sun sleeps in the garden of the sea. She turned and
faced back. The dark hills of the city were studded with lights.
It looked as if someone had swept the sky and **all** the stardust
settled into sloping clusters of people. She called the dogs and
they followed her to the truck.

Everyone works on the house and in the garden and the chicken-coop and the duckyard and the woodpile, fixing fences, pipes, wires, windows, roofs, and there is never an end to the chores and responsibilities of utopia. Sometimes the work is together and hammers bang in rhythm, shovels dig and fling in rhythm, and there is music and laughter all over. This is wonderful, this is what it's all about, work for work's sake. But then the enemy appears, the enemy outside and inside, and everyone splits, no one cares, and the garbage piles up, the bottles and cans overflow the recycling shed, and utopia becomes a dosshouse in the old Depression days. "We're too isolated," Dominic said. "It's not enough to just live here. We have to start connecting to the rest of the tribe." But how?

DOMINIC

Cockroaches and fleas multiplied like a biblical menace. He fixed one pipe and another broke, a leak in one roof stopped and another opened, and the codes of the Fire Dept., the Health Dept., the Sanitation Dept., and the Building Dept., were tacked on the board like a desert religion. Break the law and they chop your balls off. And everyone wanted to go the country. "Let's all go to the country. It's so peaceful away from the city." His vision blurred, and all the pieces of his dream stared at him like lunatic children. Every thing was falling apart and he screamed inside himself grinding his teeth. He hadn't taken a bath in two weeks and his hair and beard were knotted with sawdust and tomato sauce, and he was beginning to look heroic. But he liked the thick cheesy funk of his body. And he kept drinking at night, flopping exhausted in front of the fish. And then one night, for the first time in his life, he had a prophecy. It came in a dream all the way through thirty years, a Sunday morning his mother sending him with a dime to Borelli's Bakery, a journey into the early sun : old white wrinkled ladies always wearing black on their way to Mass, the old men playing bocceball in the alley, and the odor of black tobacco and lemon. Borelli's Bakery is stacked with warm loaves of sunshine, thick crusts of swollen shapes, long, short, stubby, bumpy, round, with holes, without holes, and how should he choose? Big bites of fullness every day, plain or with poppy seeds at lunchtime of meat balls or ham, ham and cheese, or just cheese at Calori's Delicatessen or Negrini's or Tatulli's. You might throw the cold-cuts away if they dried or the wilted lettuce sometimes when you couldn't finish, but it was a sin to throw the bread away, never throw bread away his mother said, making it holy, those big loaves she brought home with her after work to begin the evening dipped in soup. And now in the dream how should he choose? Every Sunday he'd choose a new shape Mrs. Borelli wrapped in waxed paper and tied with a string from the spool on the cracked marble counter and snapped with her thick flour-dusty fingers and clanged into the old fancy gold cash register cringading $.10 and if was his, magic food he nibbled on his way back scraping his teeth against the stub of crust so that by the time he got home there were no ends left. It was called bread, not the red, blue and yellow Wonder Silvercup Tip Top bullshit that was only good for spitballs, but the magic in back of the bakery very late at night as a teenager coming home from the pool-hall and the doors would be open and he'd wander in and buy a couple of rolls fresh from the oven. And now in the dream as he stood at the counter he didn't know how to choose. They all look so good, he said to Mrs. Borelli. I don't know which one to choose. Go in the back, she said, in the back by the oven and you can choose there. He squeezed through the racks and walked deep into not a darkness but a huge space that was very black and yet bright like shiny velvet, and glowing in the darkness Mr. Borelli like either a saint or a devil was pushing a long stick into the red mouth of the oven. The old baker stopped, looked over his shoulder as he held the long stick in the fiery womb, and then said:

— Would you like to be a baker when you grow up, little boy?

There was no honorable American bread. Money murdered all the ovens and there was no Borelli's in Berkeley. But he saw all around him, throughout all his people a great renaissance of dough rising in myriad bombs of nutrition. They were heavy, they were mealy, sometimes unleavened, full of nuts and currents and so much other stuff and often not to his personal taste, but they were worthy of the name bread, and they were a beginning.

The morning after his dream he had a visitor from the People's Bakery in Oakland. Everyone got busted in a dope; raid but the oven was still there. The barefoot visitor finished his eggs, sipped his coffee, and said:

— Would you like to be a baker?

The oven was from an old Navy ship. Solid iron. Bright yellow and black like a giant treasure chest. And from it the odor of dough would fill the streets, and flour, flour everywhere like snow, and all night long every night it would be warm beneath everyone's sleep, and in the morning there would be free bread for everyone, bread flowing in the streets like bombs of love. Please, he whispered to himself, please let it happen.

Drizzle veiled the humid night and he was passionate and sweaty as the mixers, rising pans, racks, pipes and tables were carried out to the rented U-Haul truck. He went into the rear of the storefront and looked at what was once the home of a collective, all the books, crunchy granola, revolutionary posters and remnants of the poor communards swallowed in a bust, their records and lamps and mattresses waiting to be recycled. *We'll take over for you, my brother,* he whispered to the ghost of the kitchen. The dishes in the sink, the open jar of jelly on the table, the electric clock still turning, did not answer. He stared, defying the deadly grimace of the empty furniture, and he forged in his mind the tight and solid image of thumbs, everyone's thumbs hooked to each other like !inch-pins of an axle-tree.

To take apart the oven they had to shove a long iron pivy-pole into the seam, like cave-men hunting a mammoth. The sections separated, everyone lifted with legs bent and backs straight under a thousand pounds dead weight like Egyptian slaves with blocks of stone. What engineering could conceive, will all its machinery, the capacity of a human circle? Dominic, holding the long iron pivy-pole like a spear, said:

— A lever. We could raise a city
    if we knew what levers to use.

Dominic dreams into the winter and buries himself in an oven, but mean while something else is happening. Daphne goes to the post office, Naomi works in the Food Conspiracy, Sam goes to the movies all the time, and the new year is here, but what is happening between Marian and Buster? How has it happened that they will drive to Bakerifield to get a loan from a rich relative? It's an overnight trip and there's no hurrying back.

MARIAN AND BUSTER

In February the great puddling furnace of the earth reverberates the elements, the ground stirs and all of a sudden while everyone's asleep in the winter's gloom the streets are blown with pink and gold. Plum trees veil the air with bridal lace and the acacia and scotch-broom burst bright yellow into the wet winter's dark green. Neither of them knew how their eyes suddenly entwined and drew each other in as if they both had woven a golden noose around the other's neck. The months they had known each other like polite friends suddenly dissolved and disappeared into the changing colors of the season. All the months he had watched her as mother and wife fighting with her husband and playing with her child like a Madonna and a tortured saint, all the months she had watched him come and go like a lost nomad in search of what she never knew, all the silence and walls between them suddenly gone one weekend they went on an errand as if there was nothing wrong with a married woman and lonely man being alone together.

She slipped an almond in his mouth as he drove, the dog in the back seat with the sleeping bags and the food. She said:

— *Wiltu den kernen haben, so muostu die schalen brechen.*
— What does it mean? he asked.
— It means I love almonds.

Down through the valley they rolled over the new green hills of cows and wild mustard, meadowlarks and falcons, high dramatic clouds piled above the farms in the white blue and windy morning. As he talked, his profile, his hand on the wheel, his arm out the window, recalled in her an image of a brother she never had, and in the story of his life she heard not his loneliness but her own vision of adventure, all the cities he wandered with his hands in his pockets. She said:
-I was in England that year, too.

Ten years ago. Their lives finally meeting as he discovered the girl who could have sat at his table in kindergarten. They were the same age,' meaning they were somehow equal, each other's alternative of how when they graduated school chose to travel different roads interweaving around the world to find this point, the little bubble of a Volkswagen off and on its way forever future. The years tumbled along the road like history, space opened their hearts with childhood stories of explorers and conquistadors, and their journey became blind to any destination. The highway became home, and black and white patches of cows and red dilapidated barns flew past the window as she recounted the bits and pieces of her life to this new and familiar man. And in the revelation of her past he saw the seed of the woman he had never kissed in all his life.

Over the foothills the half moon became a silver buoy floating in a sea of stars guiding them through the night. In the cold dark and secluded cabin she boiled the brown rice, fried the carrots, onions and broccoli stalks, and then put in the broccoli heads and zucchini, and in another pan friend the almonds in oil. And he sat near her and read Life Magazine and Marvel Comics left in the cabin from last summer by some family on vacation, Mommy, Daddy, Junior and Sis. They ate by candlelight, each face painted with shadows. Maybe the time for bed would not come. Their fear waited like a trial. For dessert they walked to the stuffed animal and old postcard cafe down the road. The sign read NO HIPPIES. They ordered coffee and tasteless pie and sat in the booth indifferent to the xenophobic stares of the local rednecks. Nothing could hurt them. They walked back to the cabin following the dog that led the way through the stars and the great black trees that watched over them. They had stopped talking. When they reached the cabin neither wanted to go inside. They stayed outside, under the stars. How long could they stay outside under the stars?

He said:

— I guess we'll sleep in separate beds.
— I guess so.
— We should sleep together.
—We should
—Let's sleep together.

She wasn't going to leave her husband, or was she? But she could never leave her child, or could she?

He couldn't get an erection. Naked they curled into each other deliciously cold under the heap of blankets and sleeping bags. Her body felt as deep and as dark as her eyes as he buried his face in her hair, all of him wanting to be inside her, he wanted to be inside her so much that he couldn't get an erection. She said:

— It's all right, really it's all right.

He held on, drinking her body as much as he could, praying to God: Please, God, give me a hardon. It did not come till she had fallen asleep and he had given up all hope. She woke feeling it press against her thigh. She held it gently and he kissed her gently on her lips.

They were making a circle around the golden state, from Berkeley south through the valley and over to the desert, Joshua trees and wild burros. And the next night camping in the desert under Orion's Belt, Aldebaran twinkling, ,they made love again, this time by moon set, a bluish light from the earthshine. She was crying as he came home to her, all of him spilling into a dream. She heard herself saying, she did not know why, Please don't die, my dear est, don't die. Afterwards she said:

—Buster, put on a record. Something by Perry Como or Vic Damone.

He climbed naked onto the rock above their sleeping bags and yelled *Love is a Many Splendored Thing* into the darkness, waking up all the rabbits.

Driving north on 395 she looked at the mountains and nothing was ever real, yet it moved so quickly, even the mountains moved, and as she thought fondly of her husband she held Buster's hand inside her thigh and listened to him whistle his song of the open road. He was happy. He got laid last night and life is good, it is worth living. He said:

— **One** kiss from you is worth a million dollars.

They stopped at Bishop for cookies at a Dutch bakery with cuckoo clocks. The dog was sick from too much driving and they stayed that afternoon in Bishop worrying about her as if she were their child.

They drove up into the mountains and the third night they stopped at a motel in the Sierras, snow now and tall conifers. Naked and small in the foreign motel they made love one last time and then again one last time in the morning . They opened and closed their eyes and stared at each other's wrinkles. In the stretch-marks of her flabby belly he saw the child he never had. She smelled his foul morning breath, gently closed his sorrowful lips, and kissed him as if he were a mirror. He kissed her back, kissed the imperfections of her body, her funny nose, her flabby breasts, her grey hairs, the soft, too soft and loose flesh of her arms, kissed the scars and tears of her long life, loving her with grief for all her pain and the long road of his own loneliness.

They drove north through Tahoe, turned left on 50, and stopped one last time. They parked the car at the edge of the snow and hiked into the wilderness. The morning light transformed the snow into a diaphane of dancing colors. Tufts of lichen were dazzling green upon the bark of the hemlock and juniper and the silver rocks sparkled under the bright blue sky. Everywhere became a mirror reflecting all their jeweled dreams, journey and hearth joined as they plowed knee-deep into the soft snow green silence of the wilderness. The dog leapt like a rabbit through the flurry of flakes. Then they heard a sound, like the hum of a water pump . Over the slope the sound became a roar. In the mountains the beginning of spring is no delicate maiden with blossoms in her hair. The torrents of spring are a titanic mother eating her children. Force poured into the stream from the melting snow and spilled and cracked giant boulders that lay passive under its weight. The great humps of snow crouched over the torrent like angry gods with glittering icicle teeth and spears. The source, the origin, the beginning, the prime cause, now pausing a moment in a mossy pool of last year's debris and then crashing into turbulent foam, cracking through intricate curves of rocks and carving them smooth and clean as if they were bone. Its deafening roar became death to any idyll, its terrific speed sucking all dreams into a dizzy swirl. Pick stones and fling them at the icicled teeth and spears of the malevolent fury, stop time, yell to hold back the indifferent power. But it was too beautiful, the horrible beautiful never-ending murderous mid-wife of all their love and grief, the enormous spray and churning of some big fat busy Mama's great wringer-washing machine, it was too beautiful to hold back. The two lovers walked away from the waterfall. They found a spot of quiet under a hemlock tree and they watched the dog sniff among the rocks. High very high up the tree a Stellar Jay delicately swayed a long and heavy branch loaded with snow and sprinkled snowflakes down, down upon their heads like a lullaby .

No, Buster and Marian can't be together for a happy ending. Their romance is not the end but the beginning of everything falling apart. Dominic sees it coming, the kaput of all relationships, projects, and plantations, the great demolition ball of doomsday crashing their house into another wood pile. But he will not give up and he holds on to his oven as if it could save them all.

DOMINIC

Mid-winter in Berkeley the robin's breast is speckled brown, the moss a thick carpet across the rocks, and the canopy of bay arches over a rushing stream redolent of rain and berries. The hills are deep Celtic green and all the trees tum dark. But he saw none of it this time around. His dream kept him inside, driving him like a relentless wheel as he hammered, sawed, plastered and worried about his bakery. Every morning became an emptiness, a blank page he had to fill while the pieces of the oven and all the pipes lay like fragments of a history he had to reassemble. Survey all the pieces and begin building! Full m9on's in Leo, let your life become fire, don't piss it away! Don't bother me, folks, I'm a busy man, I'm doing important work. No time for bullshit in the yard, no time to suck olives in the sun, no time to drive to Tamalpais for a hike, no time to read poetry, and no, please, no time for babies. Work. So much work. He carried his hands as if they were tools, pointing them everywhere like a master builder, quick hands he loved like he loved his mind and the feel of questions, problems to solve as ifhe were a hero. Was the floor strong enough to hold the oven? Figure it out, crawl under the house and study the founda tion. Measure lines of stress, think, think! How will it work, will wires go through the wall, will pipes fit, will people fit, will it work, the oven-rupa that will live in the middle of the city like a magical bell echoing loaves of bread like birds over the chimney pots? Harnessed to the wheels of his dream he plunged into his work on the principle he had heard all his life, repeating like an endless tape: HURRY UP HURRY UP HURRY UP. Like his heroes he hurried to work pushed by a force that made his work shop into a dungeon. Sledgehammer holes in the stone floor and fill your nose and throat with cement. Carry your dream like a bag of gravel. Scribble slogans in the wall: Make Bread Not Babies.

There is no avoiding pain, it is half of life and without it there is
no life. How could Marian and Buster build happiness together with
Theo's father jumping off the bridge? And how could Dominic bake
bread with a dead baby? Today Naomi goes to the hospital for an
abortion. And yet spring is here. Every year it comes. Of course it is
meaningless but it comes anyway.

NAOMI

After dinner and the kitchen clean and the dining room all swept and tidied she played checkers with Theo in the comer by the fish tank, while his mother and father were upstairs fighting. Under the warm ochre light of the old iron lamp the little boy resembled an angel in her dreams, a face from deep down in where, where did she know that face? Red checker in the comer jumps her black and a great belly of triumphant laughter explodes from his little hands. She looked at the miniature laughing Buddha and saw the result of a night of passion five and a half years ago. Was he her child, too, the little darling studying his checkers like Napoleon? Oh he was so cute she wanted to eat him all up, his tiny scrotum and penis, his angel eyes, his Buddha lips, she wanted to swallow him into herself and give birth to him again, her son. He was not. He was their son, the man and woman upstairs stabbing each other's eyes with hatred. And like them he would suffer, he would always carry with him the misery of his mother and father. Oh don't, I don't want you to, my little boy, my child. Suddenly she remembered where she saw that face. It was her own. In a photograph of her child hood, that magic day sitting on a pony, smiling into the black cowl of a street photographer. Me, that was me, I was that angel. Oh how happy my mother must have been to have held me in her arms. I was so beautiful. And I, will I not be a mother, too? Will I never say, My child, my darling child? Will I never hear my own child whisper in the night, Mama? Mama. Theo asked her :

    — Why are you crying?
    — I have something in my eye.
    — Let me see.
    — No, it's gone now .

In the morning daffodils and camellias filled the lawns of spring, the vines were heavy with lilac and wisteria, and everywhere she looked the joy of life stabbed her with pain. She wore her only dress, a cotton-knit print of flowers , a pair of burgundy pantyhose, and her good black boots. She curled her hair neatly in a bun, inserted her silver and turquoise earrings, and even dabbed some musk perfume on her neck. Carefully she slipped her head through the red and blue Peruvian poncho, took one last look in the mirror, and then she was ready. Her boots clicked a somber rhythm across the bare wood floor, down the stairs and out to the court yard. In the sun, her poncho flapping in the wind, she smiled to everyone that she was okay. Her two friends were waiting under the apricot tree. They would drive her to the hospital. They waved to her. They looked so beautiful and healthy. Everything was too beautiful and she could not hold back her tears. The father of her abortion kneeled at the side of the house digging to uncover the pipes. When he saw her he got up and came over, full of mud and grime, his face splattered black, his eyes twisted with guilt. She wiped the mud from his nose and his cheeks and kissed his gloomy lips. Why in the most miserable moment of her life was everything so beautiful? What game was nature playing with the zephyr wind blowing so full of joy, the halcyon trees swaying into each other as if they were making love, the robin so proud with his chest out like he was king of the universe, the daffodils so tall and triumphant as if the murder of her baby was a sacrifice to their glory? Where were the mushrooms and the slugs and the withered limbs and swollen bellies of death to pave her way to the hospital? What kind of melodrama was this, all this beauty and joy? Did tragedy not exist? Why was she not screaming? Why was she smiling and feeling so calm ? Why was everyone else smiling? Why was all the world everywhere around her smiling like the ridiculous picture of a guru, the fat folds of his silly face smiling like a pregnant belly?

I should now say PART TWO. Because several years pass and the house does fall apart and all the people inside split in different directions like a nervous breakdown. But there is really no PART TWO in the continuous flow of our lives as we move toward death. The hopes, the goals, the fantasies we shared and did not share, do not disappear as nothing really disappears but are transformed and polished like an old suffering decorated into a song. The good old years of passion and stupidity continue. Though I like to think that every seven years I'm closer to enlightenment I'm still here in the boondocks. But no story lasts forever and sooner or later we must move on to another theme. Right, Sam?

SAM

And the means by which a man lives shall be his divinity, to be worshiped and thanked for assistance. What kind of job did Sam find to save him from food-stamps and Valium? After Marian left it took a few years for him to wake wide-eyed to the great acacia tree in the yard and thank the sky for his life. He could breathe again, his lungs no longer locked with hatred and grief. After a long career of being a beatnik, a graduate student, and a bum, he finally found his life's work: Moving and Hauling. Like Norton of the Honeymooners he learned how to be happy, how to love his old truck, the sacred donkey of a Fifty-three Ford that never complained. And Sammy became a *mensch.* It meant being friendly and helpful, it meant liking people and taking care of himself, it meant putting his ad in the Classified Flea Market every two weeks and tacking business cards in laundromats and health food stores : Moving and Hauling by the Mountain Mover, cheap communist rates, call Sam, 548-1407. His son rode with him on weekends and his feelings for Marian after all these years finally settled into a love he never thought possible, he could actually love her without wanting to smash her fucking face, he could actually not want her anymore. Once in a room full of party people they paused for a moment by the refrigerator and talked like old friends. He was free of her, even in between affairs when he slept alone and remembered her in bed and enjoyed his longing to be with her again like an old childhood memory. He woke without the alarm and watered his garden and then ate a big breakfast before starting work. His clothes were clean, his house tidy as a mountain meadow, and he had not one cavity in five years. How long would this last? When would he fall into his hole again? Tomorrow had always been his most formidable enemy and now he had five maybe ten more years of this work and then he'd be too old and go back to foodstamps. Maybe he should take a vacation from feeling good and worry about the future?

He washed the dishes and took a crap and went to work. Today he loads junk from Mr. Bemheimer's garage and hauls it to the dump. What could be more pleasant? The streets were full of flowers and the smog was okay. When his father died after years of sickness his mother said: Nothing matters but health. From the dashboard radio Beethoven poured suffering into the ashtray. Everything matters. He drove through the poor section of Berkeley to the other side of the tracks and turned up Alcatraz Avenue toward the hill where the rich people live. He lifted his elbow out the window and steered with one hand and whistled along with Beethoven. It felt good not to be young and stupid anymore. Tomorrow maybe he'd be miserable again, but he could handle it. The Mountain Mover Rides Again!

Yes, Marian, there is no escape from life. Here is home or it is hell. And now that you are alone after all these years you can choose all by yourself which one you want it to be.

MARIAN

She looks for the shout of a waterfall or a loud river or wind or anything but the horror of 1-80 sucking her into the maelstrom of smog. The roar of the freeway never stops. She walked up the steps to the overpass and looked down at her sickness, the shiny diesels with skull faces of headlights and grills like furious bogies, the swarm of cars like demons that never stopped, the noise of her life that never stopped.

— I don't have to live like this.

To escape on this same highway toward the silence of birds.

— I must, I must .

Now free of husband and lover, and her child old enough, she could pack her bag and leave Berkeley and its pacifying flowers and tickytacks that were no different from any other city, leave the familiar faces of the same old strangers in the Co-op and the cafés, leave the center for new therapies and religions, the secluded shelter under the radiation lab perched on the hill like a pyramid of priests, leave her old friends of nothing in common anymore, leave her Marian cottage and her Marian plants and Marian kitchen and all her Marian art and junk she never stopped accumulating like an old maid and a show-off, leave her journals and her mailbox and go somewhere in Idaho or Arizona where she could be unhappy with birds instead of automobiles. But the noise was everywhere and wherever she ran it would appear like fungus always grows on anything dying, highways and wires that spread everywhere and someday all over the galaxy, the roads of her escape she could never get off. Often unable to sleep she would lie in the darkness in the middle of the night and listen to the drone of the freeway as if it were the pulse of life itself, the drone of all humanity that never stopped going somewhere. She had lived in Berkeley for fifteen years and had wanted to leave it for fifteen years. She left it for a year, a summer, a weekend, always returning as if it held a noose around her neck. And now at the age of thirty-seven she crossed over her enemy, passed the fruit and vegetable vendor by the traffic from .the racetrack, and then walked to the marina. Here the drone of· the freeway stopped, the western wind blowing it back to the city where it was born as if the water did not want it. And she rested in the quiet of the rocks and listened to tinkling of the sailboats that reminded her of donkey bells long ago in a Spanish village once when she was happy, and like a donkey she felt weary and peaceful. Then she strolled to the pier. Here the wind was strong and loud and she watched the scooters bob in the waves, rising and dipping indifferently to the turbulence of the high tide. The sun was almost down and the pier was full of people fishing. The light was the soft color of her most happy dreams, a renaissance light of the bay of Saint Francis and the blue hills that roll into it like a gentle serpent. The long rays painted quiet silhouettes of the people fishing and swallowed the misery that had driven her here. And, as if recuperating from a deep illness, she felt very slow and open and now nothing mattered but that the noise in her head was gone and she was ready to see the boy standing by the sink where the fish were cut and cleaned. The dying light turned him into gold. She saw him all of a sudden and felt as if he had been waiting for her. And he was smiling as if he remembered her from another life. At first she became afraid, and then she saw that he was retarded. He was a mulatto child, about ten years old, in very clean clothes and new white sneakers, standing very still as if he were about to be photographed. And in his smile she recognized what she had feared all her life not only for her own child but all that she held most important in her mirror, the thin pin of her mind slipping out and leaving her helpless with no Marian for defense. He gazed up at her as if he loved her, as if she were his mother. Then a woman who probably was his mother called him, "Michael! Michael!" And in the stink of fish, amid the guts of their slaughter, with the scavenger seagulls suspended in the air above them like ambiguous angel, he waved goodbye, the little idiot saint alone in the dim light of his defective life, carving in her eyes a smile from the prison of the world he could never leave, smiling as if to lay himself at the mercy of a power he could never even consider challenging. And in the caw of gulls, in the loud blasting wind from the sea, she heard the roar of the freeway, the lion roar of a bodhisattva, the violent churning of a noisy ocean. And into this chaos she whispered, "Bye, Michael, bye-bye, little boy," and she curled her fingers as if caressing his face, smiling back to that face with her own feeble-minded joy that came from nowhere and would return to nowhere.

As we grow older we think more and more of sickness and death not morbidly or with fascination but with gratitude that they have spared us at least this far. And is not gratitude the first step toward JOY, Buster. But how often do we ignore our good fortune, my stupid Buster who goes off alone again, though you are never as alo11e as you think. For the an el of death is always with you, the guardian angel who protects you until the final moment.

However neatly he trims the hair in his nose, however precisely he dental-flosses, or however many times he shakes his wang so no leftover drops will stain his pants, Buster is a careless and sloppy man. But what does it matter in the mountains where nothing is dirty, where even the marmot turds are food for his dog, Lulu, who chews them like little fudge bars. This garden as clean as a monastery and the snow everywhere an infant loveliness, a gift especially for him with no mosquitoes or other campers. Lulu barked and circled and leaped into the snow as if it were the return of Mommy. The lake was still frozen but Buster found a patch of dry ground near a stream and he made his home here with his plastic orange tent and his blue backpack and a pile of firewood snug and dry like an island paradise, *Buster's Hole In The Snow*. He fed Lulu three handfuls of chunk-style dog food on a rock, and then he started a fire and dried his shoes and socks. Then, with impeccable organization, he prepared dinner. He boiled the bulgur on one side of the grill and on the other fried the carrot and onion and zucchini which was worth carrying because it was so much better than that freeze-dried crap. He even brought along a little curry and wondered how far the odor would drift. He had timed it just right and would drink his green tea with a full stomach exactly with the sunset. Ah, such an organizer . Already two days and a night up here and he was swollen with perfection. Were the people who owned houses on the lower lake some kind of mafia rich enough to live up here? How come them and not everyone?

— I want to be here forever. I don't want to go back.

And that night by the fire he was perhaps happier than he had ever been, and he sat in the hollow of the old juniper tree that sheltered him from the wind, and he watched the fire and the moon and the stars and he listened to the water and the wind, and there was no one with him except Lulu but Lulu was now more of the wilderness, and even when he tried to remember a woman his solitude pushed her away and he was satisfied with his life. He finished his second cup of hot chocolate and burped. Then he pulled his clothes off and scrambled into the sleeping bag and into the warmth of his own body. He felt so good he tried to keep his eyes open and hold off sleep for as long as he could.

— Dear life, thank- you.

In the morning he was still happy, and after his crunchy granola and coffee had a wonderful shit crouching monkey-posture gazing at the great white pyramids of mountain-tops shining in the early sun. Then he went on his hike, leaving his jacket at the camp because he would be back before sundown, and he filled his shirt pockets with almonds and raisins for lunch. Look, folks, look at Buster in his short pants and faded flannel shirt in the middle of snow thousands of feet above the nearest pollution. And look, look at the incredible lodgepole and hemlock and how the deeper you walk into the wilderness the more beautiful they become, their branches rising into the blue like a revelation. There were no trails and Lulu walked behind him as they went further into the silence and the light, up and over in the general direction of the next lake. They came to a meadow and he crossed it like a little boy wandering tip-toe into a forbidden temple, overwhelmed by its sudden beauty. But it was not until they climbed the crest and came down to the next lake that he entered the sanctum sanctorum of this great temple, with two mountains on either side, one a little higher than the other, like god and goddess, and the dead trees rising out of the blue and green ice like silver ruins of an ancient civilization . He found a shady spot by a little trickle of melting snow and a dry root stump to sit on while he ate his nuts and raisins and flipped

Lulu an almond every now and then. For dessert he drank from the melting snow, the beverage of the gods, that costs money in the super market. And when he had enough pleasure he decided to go back. The sun was past noon but still hot. He was getting more and more tan. He would look like a hotshot woodsman. He tucked in his manly faded shirt, tied his wet and heroic old boots, and gathered himself into a neat bundle for his hike back, somewhere over there not too far, a few clouds but nothing to worry about, whistling, this altogether perfect human being, the zenith of multi cellular evolution, looking for his footsteps back. Lulu followed him like the dog in the Tarot pack follows the fool. And in his sloppy enthusiasm and stupid exhilaration Buster got lost. He lost his footsteps. Altogether happy, whistling the song of himself, he came to a meadow, but it was not the same meadow. He stopped whistling. He looked around and then it took approximately half a second for fear to grip his throat and strangle him. Poor stupid Buster, a child lost in his careless wandering, on trails that look so much like home but are not home. Someone died up here a month ago, frozen to death. Clouds filled the sky and no more sun. The trees became indifferent. And the snow began to smile that old familiar LSD smile: Hello, Buster, so we meet again. He ran. He ran back toward where he thought he had just been. But he was not thinking straight. He was no longer Buster of the neat nose and clean wang. There was no more room in this temple for a phony. He kept running, his lungs very painful now, a painful knot in his side, running as if to escape from his own fear and panic. He ran toward where he thought there might be some other campers. There were none. He ran up the crest to find somewhere familiar but at the crest he saw a different lake and a different meadow, and he ran back to get back to the second place and came to a third place even more terrible. He couldn't feel his legs anymore and his hands and face were numb and he was now in hell, running nowhere, choking, and delirious. And he fell into a hole, the snow caving under him, covering him up to his shoulders. He was now crying and Lulu licked his face. He tried to yell but he had no breath left and his voice was feeble.

— Help!

Help, as if the marmots and the chipmunks would come and save him. Please, he cried, please stop fooling around, I want to go home. Eventually Buster does get home, he doesn't die yet, he doesn't even get frostbite, he goes on wandering through the story of his life until his guardian angel becomes his angel of death. But now, this moment in the middle of his journey, in short pants and suntan like an ignorant tourist with only his head and shoulders above ground and Lulu who knew nothing of death licking his tears as if this were all a game, now is the moment of Buster's freakout and crack-up as all the helps in his life come together in this one whimpering feeble help.

— Oh please help me.

Now, Buster, now look at the snow and the trees and see them like your nose hair in the mirror that will keep growing in your grave with no one to cut them. Now look at the mountains which are not gods or temples. Now carry a compass and a map for the rest of your life instead of a mirror and a camera. This wilderness is not your garden, not yet and perhaps never, not until you are equal to it and the sunset isn't timed to your dinner. He pushed himself up but was now too exhausted to keep running. He felt sick and wanted to lie down and close his eyes. But there were only about two hours till darkness. Somehow, he didn't know how, he found the strength to keep moving. Now there was nothing but the desperate moving to find another, that other whom he had needed all his life and ran away from all his life. He was not looking for landmarks anymore, only people. There were some, he had met them earlier. And whether they were fascists or mafia or bullshitters or whatever didn't matter, he had to find them and throw himself at their feet and kiss their feet and save him self or he would die. The trees would not save him, the mountains would not save him, they did not care. Even his beloved Lulu did not care and would even eat his dead flesh if need be. He moved on, homing toward his own kind, toward his family wherever they were, however ugly or boring. And he finally found two young hikers camped by a lake. He tried to hold himself together when he approached their tent but as soon as he started to speak to them he burst into tears. So happy to see them, so relieved and exhausted, he sat on a rock near their fire and cried. They were almost young enough to be his children. They looked at him and were silent. An hour later, after one of them directed him back to his camp like a big brother holding his hand across the street, he returned to his footsteps. Dazed, numb, and wiped out, he entered Buster's Hole In The Snow. The orange tent, the blue pack, the pots, and the juniper tree were the same as if nothing had happened. He could have died and they would still be here. Lulu curled on a rock and immediately went to sleep. He drank some water from the stream and then fell to his knees and vomited. He curled and bowed his head as if he were being baptized. And water and bile and the bullshit of his life spilled into the snow as he retched and gasped. And that night he sat in the hollow of the juniper tree and stared at the fire, stupid and ashamed, small and thankful.

What is the price of experience, Naomi? Can you buy it for a song? Or wisdom for a dance in the street? Suffering is the best teacher. And she who is awake lifts her wings and does not stay in the old homes of karma. My child, my little girl, you are your own child, your own daughter and son, many daughters and sons, each one a tear from your grief, all your pain returning from heaven with the angels of birth.

NAOMI

In the great valley of California the summer evening opens her heart to stars and the meaning of life. Finally on a farm with tomatoes and com and the old owl who lives in the palm tree and all the animals, there is no more holding on, no clinging. She works hard, goes to bed early and wakes with the rooster and the red dawn. And now the harvest moon peeps over the hill. The kitchen smells of chocolate cookies and some of the others are smoking dope and eating everything in sight. But the voluptuous night pulls her out side and she walks down the road by the canal toward nothing but acres and acres of vineyard after vineyard. For wine. And whatever wine is for. Back in Berkeley the streets are cold with fog and streetlights. She couldn't take it anymore and left after the abortion, finding new friends in the valley and no more noise. She missed those who stayed on, and alone now on the road toward nothing she sent them not clinging but a nod and a smile that though she may never see them again they never leave her. All her life she longed for a family, longed for it more than sex or power, longed for brothers, sisters and children as a lost child desperately cries for a mother or father . Her vision of paradise had been every one she ever loved together for Thanksgiving dinner and music and dance. Instead she had always been dubious of love and made friends with caution. Now she looked at the stars as if they were her friends and asked their forgiveness: I'm sorry. I'm sorry not for my needs but that I never let you look in my eyes. Everywhere the night lay awake, the moon as bright as Yankee Stadium and the crowd of crickets as loud as her desire. There were too many beloved to fit in one place for Thanksgiving dinner. Too many years to resolve in a moment. Unless she could open her arms and forgive the stars for all her pain, let go of her loneliness and forgive life for the child she never had. Unless she lie in the cool evening powder of the valley soil and slowly open her wound and lie vulnerable to a shower of light.

Unless she marry the stars that would become a protoplasmic mass of streaming bubbles, particles of memory suffused with light, light in a slow coil through her wound as if light were the child conceived inside the undulating yawn of her thighs, a power writhing and spreading up into the region of her heart and filling the emptiness there and forcing the grief and guilt out of her eyes forever. She had hated not only her own life but every star that seemed to smile at her suffering, and now they returned to her love as she cried from deep in her joy asking forgiveness, forgiving them for their mystery, opening her wound and letting them enter like all the friends she never embraced.

What can we make of all our failures, Dominic? Are they compost for salvation? 0 my hero, the failure, undefeated by success, driving home to that horizon that can never be reached, is failure the goal of all your struggling?

DOMINIC

How lovely the curves the flies carve in the air and the way they scratch themselves with their feet, and who cares if they eat shit, he loved them. Yet he killed flies and he not only killed fleas and mosquitoes but squeezed and smashed them to death like Hitler. And he used to kill the cute mice that stared at him from under neath the refrigerator, and once he killed his own child. And when he was a kid he used to pound the pillows like Joe Palooka, *pow wham socko* his enemies and kill them dead. And now he stood at the barbed wire fence and talked to the gentle calf with the big baby eyes of guilt.

— I eat you once a week in spaghetti sauce.

But the calf stared back and forgave him: you're a good person, Dominic, you're okay. He was on his way back to Berkeley from a trip up north, and he had stopped here to take a piss. Pissing into the earth he felt himself decaying, pulled down and wanting to die: Dear Naomi, my dreams have made me sick. I wanted to make something of my life and give it to the world as if I were a hero. Now nothing is more important than death. He sat under the wide branches of an old stone pine and crossed his legs and closed his eyes and watched the rise and fall of his breath. People came on and off the movie screen of his eyelids like a farce. He remembered once driving up Dwight Way in Berkeley when he saw an old man drop his pants and shit in the middle of the sidewalk. No one would clean it because the sidewalk was by an empty lot and he wondered whether anyone walking by would notice if it were dog shit or human shit. Nothing ever came of the oven. After everyone moved out, a collective from San Francisco came and took it away. He was forty years old. It was not as if he could say, Well, I'm young and it's the nature of youth to dream and fail. Yet nothing changed. He was still the same nineteen year old kid hating fascists. And one day he'd wake up an old hermit with utopia on his walls like toilet graffiti. The tall May green grass was just beginning to yellow. He sank into it and lay on his back and sucked a daisy stem staring up at the high branches waving in the wind like hallucinations. All his life he hated people, especially scumbags. He saw them eating Safeway hamburger and shitting in the middle of civilization, old disease-mongers who died snoring. A ladybug crawled on his hand telling him to stop. Stop, Dominic, stop hating. Ishi lived in these hills fishing and hunting. There are more Ishis than scumbags in the world, there has to be. He remembered many years ago when as a messenger boy in Manhattan he worked with an old bum named Minasche. One morning Minasche came to work with a big wet spot on his fly. His usual dirty white shirt smelled like baloney. The boss said, "Dominic, ask Minasche to go home and change his pants." So he said, "Minasche, your pants are wet." Minasche said, "I know, I pissed in them. Sometimes when I sneeze I can't hold it back." Minasche of the tiny blue eyes and the Santa Claus belly, who waddled down the street with one shirt-tail in and the other shirt-tail out, an extremely good man, ridiculous, kind, and gentle. And he loved him. And as the years passed he knew many more Minasches. They filled his life with dirty shirts and twinkling noses. He said so-long to the calf and the old stone pine and the tall grass and the ladybug and he got back in the car and continued driving through the land and the history of people. He was too old to keep hating them. I love people he said to the landscape, as I love Minasche's baloney armpits. Give me your lumpen bums and I will build the celestial city. He was dreaming again, only this time he would not fight, he would not struggle, he would be more like the otter than the beaver. He would enjoy himself and swim in the shitty river of life doing what he could like an old Wobbly in the woods. And his new dream billowed with the cloud curled above the hills and the clear horizon. I will never give in to you, he said to whatever it was inside him and outside him that tried to pull him down. He remembered a story his mother told him. On the ship from Naples there was a boy, Nunzio, who told her, "I'll never work. Do you think I'm going to America to shine shoes? Never." Nunzio, the gambler. He remembered him only as an old man with white socks and a cane , but it was true, he never worked a day in the new country and lived better than most. There were at least ten thousand bums in Berkeley. With a little dreamstuff they could do anything. And out of the carbuncles of a hopeless heap of failures could come another Goya or a Beethoven with rotten teeth and bad breath and deafness curled above the hills like a dancing elephant.

So long, Daphne, my old girl, my sweetheart. See you when you get back. I would say good luck but is luck ever good or bad? The bedbugs, the dysentery, the weariness and misery that await you will become when you return even more joyful than the good times. And you will look back to every step of your journey as you look back to your childhood all bundled up on the way to Grandma's house when you sat in back of the car and stared out the window at the cinema of life.

DAPHNE

When she was a little girl she used to stand on the hill of her hometown and look out over the marsh to the small blue mountains at the edge of the world. The word *America* always meant crossing those mountains. Even as a woman when she became political, *America* meant land more than money or murder, a giant full of geography and exotic strangers. And now on the highway across her childhood the sign read:

> THE NEXT EXIT
> HAS NO SERVICES

She remembered standing on a hill in the clarity of a morning washed clean in the aftermath of a storm, purple and orange adventure clouds resting over the small dark bumps of the local mountains, the little river squirming across the marsh. And in her mind the scene became an image of what *America* was like out there all clean and quiet. But now, driving across reality, somewhere in Utah, she picked up a boy just back from the war. A navigator in a bomber who became a junkie in Thailand. "I guess," he said, 'Tm responsible for killing about fifty thousand people." He was a good boy, from Arkansas, and was shy and she might have slept with him. The clouds dropped massive shadows across the landscape. In Iowa she rested in a cozy motel with a hot shower and television, and in the morning rejoiced with hashbrowns and over easy. In Ann Arbor she considered staying with a man and postponing her trip. In Maine the cry of the loon came from the unexplored. She was too young to die in Berkeley. Sooner or later she'd go back, but not tomorrow. She remembered one very rare night at the house when Buster made ice-cream with fresh pineapple in the old ice-cream maker in the kitchen and brought it up to her room to offer her some and she said, "Stay for a while, Buster." Sam and Marian were not fighting then and Naomi and Dominic were okay too and all their bedroom doors were open. One person led to another and before she knew it they were all sitting around her bed smoking dope. And she fell asleep listening to them and iii the morning they were still there, snoring in a circle. Maybe she will never see them again but they will always be with her. She was flying high now, and long like the swan, stopping at the flyways for a look around and then on her way again. Marian was from Pennsylvania, Buster from New Jersey, Sam from Massachusetts, Naomi from Illinois, and Dominic from New York. Now she had been to all those places. But she had never been to Istanbul. Or to Calcutta.

Today a letter came from a friend across the ocean. He has been in jail for more than a year and still no trial. Every day he waits in a little cell with no sky and longs to see the sun. He writes: "Amigo. I received your last letter and when I touched the yellow paper it brought me back to my childhood which had faded like your paper but now comes back so clear in this place. This place. You ask me what it's like, and I tell you, old pal, it's a living death. It's a night without morning, and potatoes. Lots of potatoes. I'm a prisoner but they feed me potatoes. They say this prison is considered humane and this country is humane and clean of history. But here inside is the stink of sweat and potatoes, and here is where the shit comes, the dregs, the losers, the ones who are unconnected, unloved, lost. And every morning at 6:30 a loudspeaker cracks our sleep and we get up for no reason. One fellow said to me the other day, 'I thought some things were normal, but I see now there is no normal.' He's a cross-eyed Israeli who was born in Afghanistan and somehow made his way here. I also met an Armenian who told me a secret. He said Armenians were biding their time and waiting for the inevitable invasion of Turkey. He swears revenge but he's sixty years old and still here. When I first saw him I said, 'You're no Greek.' (He's supposed to be Greek.) He agreed, 'Yes, I am an Armenian.' And then there is the Bolivian who says when he reaches the age of fifty he will become a revolutionary but in the meanwhile he's just an ordinary thief. But to get back to your yellow paper: often while I'm sitting here I smell something or hear something and the memories come flooding in. Ordinary things that had seemed unimportant. Like eating dinner on the Sabbath with my family, the smell of chicken on Friday evenings, or the endless afternoons playing games with my brother, monopoly, all-star baseball. Then it stops, and I look at the walls. These walls that feel like I have died and the years come in and out and there is no one home, just an awareness. And all of a sudden I laugh. This miserable place and the voices screaming in the night are so painful that I laugh and I'm not sure if I'm really laughing or crying. And yet, my friend, as I write to you now I realize that I'm still alive, and over the past year I have come to understand myself more deeply. Someday I'll be out of this place. I'll be back in America taking money in and out of a bank, driving a fancy car and living in a big house with lemon trees in the backyard. And the Israeli and the Armenian and the Bolivian will still be here. And I feel that as long as they are here a part of me will always be here too. And this feeling makes me cry. It opens my heart and fills me with love, and I realize that we are all prisoners in this life, we are all together . . . ."

My story stops here for a while. But there is more to come. My friend and Dominic, Naomi, Marian, Sam, Buster, Daphne, all have their future in Theo, the child. When all of me comes together then will that child end my story and sing the song of transfiguration. But for now that boy plays by himself in the distance. That silky haired, soft-eared, awkward innocent is the child Naomi wanted to feed and dress, the child that Marian knew outside herself but not inside herself, the child that Buster and Sam murder ed in their doubt and hopelessness, the child Dominic wanted not in flesh but in the founding of a city, the child Daphne would find in her voyage around the world. Is this child doomed? Will he become another sad story? Or is he the radiant eternal child waiting for us at the shore? There he is in back of the orchestra, next to the captain on the ferryboat. And the gulls are not cawing over garbage but dipping and rising like angels within the vaulted dome of this prison, of this home within a home.

www.ingramcontent.com/pod-product-compliance
Lightning Source LLC
Chambersburg PA
CBHW031955130726
47904CB00013B/2318